THE TROUBLE
WITH
HERBERT

HEATHER EYLES

Illustrated by WENDY SMITH

This edition published in the United States of America in 1997
by MONDO Publishing
First published in Great Britain in 1989 by Hutchinson Children's Books,
an imprint of Random House UK Limited

For information contact:
MONDO Publishing,
980 Avenue of the Americas,
New York, NY 10018

Printed in the United States of America
First Mondo printing, November 1996
00 01   9 8 7 6 5 4 3

Library of Congress Cataloging-in-Publication data
Eyles, Heather.
    The trouble with Herbert / Heather Eyles ; illustrated by Wendy
Smith.
        p.   cm.
    Summary: Herbert the guinea pig provides a series of adventures for
a class of second graders and their teacher.
    ISBN 1-57255-218-2 (pb : alk. paper)
    [1. Schools—Fiction. 2. Guinea pigs—Fiction.] I. Smith, Wendy,
ill. II. Title.
PZ7.E974Tr   1996
[E]—dc20   96-15047
                                                          CIP
                                                          AC

Contents

One

Here is The Class,

and here is Ms. Bagnall,
their teacher.

The children call her Baggy
Pants, but not when she can
hear them!

Here are some interesting
members of The Class:

Colin Crybaby,

who is always crying about
nothing.

Biffo the Bully,

who is always making Colin cry.

Rachel Rushaway,

the fastest girl in the school.

And Brian Brainbox, the
smartest boy in the world.

He really is the smartest boy in
the world.(Someone has to be.)

And there are lots, lots more.
Here they are, all trying to speak
at once.

The Class has a guinea pig
called Herbert.

He will be very important later
in this book. He likes eating,
especially corn and carrots.
Watch out!

Two

This chapter is the story of Fred,
The Class's corn plant,
who grew from a seed,

to a shoot,

to a baby corn plant,

to a great big bushy
plant.

The children watered Fred, fed
him, polished him until he
shone,

and showed him to all of their
visitors.

One day something knobby
poked out of Fred's side.

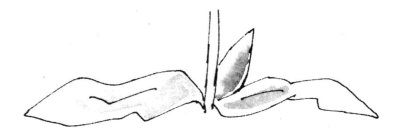

It grew bigger and bigger
every day until it was a great
big corn on the cob,

with a feathery top.

The children were very proud
of Fred. They made a card for
him,

and they all signed it in their
best handwriting.

The whole school came to see
Fred.

"Now," said Baggy Pants
(sorry, Ms. Bagnall), "when
are we going to eat him?"

"EAT HIM?" cried the children.
"OH, NO!"

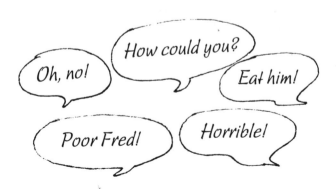

Colin Crybaby burst into tears,

as usual.

That started off Biffo the Bully,

as usual.

But everyone else felt like crying, too.

That afternoon, Rachel
Rushaway was in charge of
giving Herbert the guinea pig
his food.

She was in such a hurry, as
usual, that she left the door of
his cage open.

It was open
only
a tiny bit,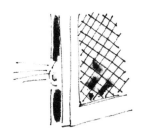

but it was just enough for
Herbert to get his nose through.

He sniffed. He wiggled.
He pushed.

He was out!

Here is Herbert,

always hungry.

Here is Fred,

ready to be eaten.

The next morning, The Class was very quiet when Baggy Pants (sorry, Ms. Bagnall) came in.

she asked.

Silence. Not a word.

she said.

Silence.

The children pointed to Fred.

Then they pointed to Herbert.

Herbert looked very fat. And
sleepy.

He was smiling.

"Ah," said Ms. Bagnall. "I see. Well, that's what plants are for, you know. For eating."

Colin started to cry.

Biffo pinched Rachel.

Rachel started to cry.

The whole class started to cry.

Then Baggy Pants (sorry,
Ms. Bagnall) started to cry.

"Why are you crying, Ms.
Bagnall," asked Brian Brainbox,
"if plants are for eating?"

"Because I wanted to eat him myself," said Ms. Bagnall, "with lots of butter!"

POP!

Herbert looked very smug.

Three

This chapter is about Herbert again.

Now, when Herbert escaped that day, he found he liked it.

Every chance he got, he was out of his cage again and on his way.

He would find a hole to crawl
into,

a corner to hide in,

a blanket to crawl under.

HERBERT
SHAPED

The next day the children
would have to look for him—

over,

under,

beside.

They always found him in
the end.

One day Herbert was bored.

Fed up.

He hadn't escaped in a long time. He looked around. His cage was not locked.

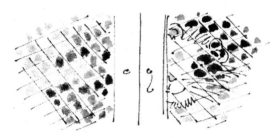

He looked again. The classroom door was open.

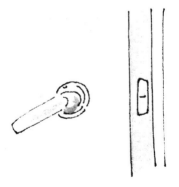

Just a crack!

He looked a third time. The
children were busy.

No one was looking at Herbert.
Everyone was working hard.

Herbert squeezed out of his
cage,

DOWN THE TABLE LEG,

AND OUT OF THE DOOR

Suddenly Brian Brainbox, who had finished his math first (he always did), shouted,

Herbert!
He's escaped!

There was pandemonium.
(That means a lot of noise.)

Rachel Rushaway, the fastest girl in the school, flew after Herbert.

She ran, *ZOOM*
OUT OF
THE DOOR, *DOWN THE FRONT STAIRS*

RUSH

- CRASH -

OUT OF THE SCHOOL DOORS, AND

'ROUND AND 'ROUND THE PLAYGROUND.

But she didn't catch Herbert.
Herbert hadn't gone that way.

Herbert had gone

to sleep.

Brian Brainbox thought he
knew where Herbert was.

This is what he thought:

Guinea pigs like 1. Food
                      2. More food
                      3. Warmth
                      4. Comfort
                      5. Yet more
                           food

He was right, of course!
Herbert, always hungry, had
smelled delicious smells.

SNIFF
SNIFF

He had followed his nose

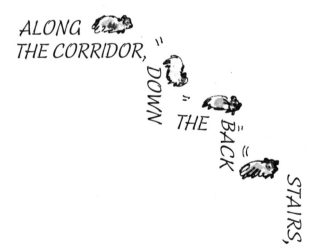

*ALONG
THE CORRIDOR,*
*DOWN
THE BACK
STAIRS,*

and into the kitchen, where the
cooks were cooking lunch.

He licked his lips.

He could smell his second
favorite food.

Carrots! Yummy carrots!

Piles and piles of them.

The cooks were busy making a pie for lunch.

They didn't see Herbert.

He began to eat.

He ate,

and he ate,

and he ate,

until he could eat no more.
Then he fell asleep.

Just then, The Class, led by
Brian Brainbox, rushed through
the kitchen door.

He's very fat.

Have you seen
our Herbert?

And brown.

"I know he's here," said Brian
Brainbox. "He likes corn and
carrots." CARROTS!

 The cooks looked.

Brian looked.
The children looked.

"Herbert!"

He'd eaten all the carrots. Piles and piles of them.

They were all gone.

shrieked one cook,

"Pardon me," said Brian.
"Herbert's not a rat, he's a . . ."

Herbert moved. "Stop him!"
someone shouted. "He's trying
to get away!"

But Herbert was now too

F A T

to run anywhere.

He was soon back in his cage.

Baggy Pants (sorry, Ms. Bagnall) got a new padlock for Herbert's cage,

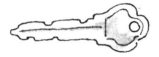

and only she had the key.

She kept it in the top right-hand drawer of her desk.

KEY

This fact is important for the next chapter.

By the way, Rachel Rushaway wasn't still whizzing 'round the playground.

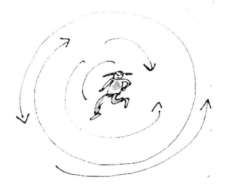

When Herbert was found, she made her way back to the classroom. Very quickly.

Four

The sky was blue,

the sun was shining,

and The Class was miserable.

"It's much too nice to stay indoors everyday," said Baggy Pants. "Let's go on a picnic this week."

Herbert thought that was a good idea.

"But Herbert has to stay behind," she added.

Biffo the Bully had other ideas.

Biffo knew where Ms. Bagnall kept the key to Herbert's cage.

On the day of the picnic, the
bus arrived.

Twenty-five children got on the
bus with twenty-five lunch
boxes.

LUNCH

MORE
LUNCH

EVEN
MORE
LUNCH

Baggy Pants got on
(sorry, Ms. Bagnall).

The bus driver
got on,

and so did Herbert,

in Biffo's pocket.

Herbert started to squeak with excitement.

SQUEAK
SQUEAK

"Be *quiet*, Herbert," said Biffo. "You'll get me into trouble."

But The Class was singing so loudly, nobody heard Herbert.

Row, row, row your boat...

At last they came to a beautiful
park, with trees, and swings,

and hills to roll down,

and best of all, a wonderful
boating lake.

Everyone wanted to go boating,

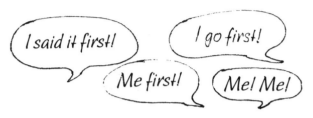

except Colin Crybaby.

Boo hoo!

said Colin. "I don't like water, and I don't like lakes, and I don't like boats."

"All right," said Ms. Bagnall. "You can sit here and watch over the lunch boxes."

So he did. All twenty-five of
them.

TWENTY-SIX
(MS. BAGNALL'S)

The Class got into the biggest
boat on the lake and Baggy
Pants (sorry, Ms. Bagnall)
rowed them all out into the
middle of the lake.

We're off!

Hooray!

But someone was still hiding in Biffo's pocket.

Herbert was beginning to feel hungry, as usual. He could smell his second-favorite food (carrots, of course) in Rachel Rushaway's pocket, all the way at the other end of the boat.

Herbert wriggled out of Biffo's pocket,

and ran along the side of the boat.

A life on the ocean wave!

"EEEEEEEEKKKKKKKK!" shouted Baggy Pants. "A rat! A rat on board!"

Ms. Bagnall wasn't expecting to see Herbert. She thought he was still locked up in his cage. To her he looked just like a BIG, FAT RAT.

Why does everyone think I look like a rat?

"EEK!" shouted Rachel Rushaway, who didn't know what she was shouting at. She hadn't seen Herbert.

"EEK! EEK!" shouted all the children, who hadn't seen anything either.

 *Zoom!*

went Rachel, over to the other side of the boat.

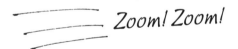 *Zoom! Zoom!*

went all the children, to get away from the rat that was really Herbert.

When twenty-five (sorry, twenty-four) children and a teacher stand on one side of a boat, something happens.

That's right.

They all landed in the water.

Luckily, the water wasn't very
deep, only up to their waists.
But they all got very wet,

including Ms. Bagnall.

Back on shore they all dripped
and shivered.

"Blast that rat!" said Baggy
Pants who was shivering most
of all.

REALLY
BIG →
SHIVERS

"Please, Ms. Bagnall," said Biffo. "That wasn't a rat. That was Herbert. And he's . . . and he's . . ."

Biffo started to cry.

"Boo hoo!" cried Biffo. "Boo hoo!" All the children started to cry with him.

Except Colin. Colin didn't cry
at all. Instead he walked into
the water

up to his shoes,

then up to his knees,

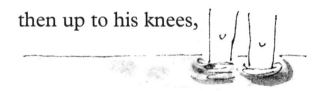

then up to his waist,

and then he bent down and
completely disappeared!

The Class cried even harder.
There was no sign of Colin.

NO COLIN

Then suddenly, out of the
water came first one arm,

then another

with something in its hand.
Something wet, and brown, and
fat, looking like a rat.

"It's . . . HERBERT!" cried the
children. "Colin saved him!"
"Hooray for Colin!"
"Three cheers for Colin!"

So Colin changed his name.

And that's the end of the story.
Well, not quite.

Biffo doesn't bully anymore (well, hardly).

Rachel doesn't run *quite* as quickly (but still quickly enough).

Herbert stays in his cage (with plenty of corn and carrots).

Brian is still the smartest boy in the world (really and truly).

And The Class still calls Ms. Bagnall Baggy Pants (and sometimes she can hear them).

GOODBYE!